· FOR ·

David, Zak, and Hannah.

When Ellie found a magic well,
her wishes all came true.

Come, follow her adventures
and enjoy them with her, too!

OH, ELLIE!

 Amanda Kidd

 Noor Alshalabi

Cuckoo-Bye House Publishers

Mel the Mole watched as his friend Ellie placed a cupcake on the ground, then threw a coin into the wishing well.

In a burst of fizzy sparkles, Ellie began to shrink.

She became **smaller**...

and **smaller**...

until she was the size of a mouse.

"Look, Mel. My wish came true!" Ellie said.

In all the excitement, she didn't notice the cupcake...

being lifted onto
tiny shoulders and...

WHOOSH!

"Ants!" yelled the mole,
pointing at the thieves.

Ellie watched in dismay as the insects
ran off with their find, disappearing
between dewy blades of grass.

"Why did you make yourself so small?" asked Mel. "Don't you know how fast ants run?"

Ellie explained that when she'd used a wish to turn into a giant, cupcakes seemed tiny. "So, whenever I want a ginormous cupcake, I make myself smaller."

Mel scratched his head. "Can you not wish for a giant cupcake instead?"

Oh, Ellie!

Suddenly, Ellie felt silly and wanted to reverse her wish. But that's really hard to do when...

... the well is as big as a **mountain!**

Ellie huffed and puffed as she climbed the cobblestones, using twigs and leaves to pull herself up.

By the time she reached the top,
her knees were grazed, her face was red,
and the coin had fallen out of her pocket.

Oh, Ellie!

Ellie groaned and stamped her feet, but the only thing she could do was climb back down.

"Being tiny is hard," she muttered.

A loud **"CAW"** startled them both.

Ellie forgot about the coin as she and Mel slipped inside the molehill to hide.

SWOOP!

Just like that, the coin was gone, soaring high in the sky in the clutches of a delighted magpie.

"No way!" Ellie cried. "How will I get back? I have no coins left, and I'm too tiny to walk all the way home!"

Luckily, Mel had a bright idea.
"These tunnels lead straight to your garden. Follow me," he said.

Ellie liked the thought of sneaking back home underground. However, she soon changed her mind.

The burrows were dark. **Eep!**

And smelly. **Pee-yew!**

Even worse, they were full of wiggly worms. **Yuck!**

Ellie thanked Mel for his help
and hauled herself out at the
next molehill.

She was too busy shaking the soil
out of her hair to notice the kestrel
hovering overhead.

SNATCH!

The bird flew to her nest and plopped
Ellie inside, where two hungry chicks
were eagerly waiting.

"Why is our breakfast wearing a dress?"
chirped one of the chicks.

"I'm not your breakfast!"
said Ellie, and she told
them her story.

"You'll never make it home on your own," said the kestrel. "Hop onto my back, and we'll be there in no time."

The pair flew over woods and houses before landing in Ellie's garden. Ellie waved goodbye to her new friend and sprinted toward her parents.

Dad was startled when he spotted something rustling through the grass.

"Mouse!" he shrieked, throwing a shoe at Ellie.

"Dad!" she squeaked as he ran inside and hid under the bed.

Mum laughed and extended an open palm. "Ellie, sweetheart. Is that you?"

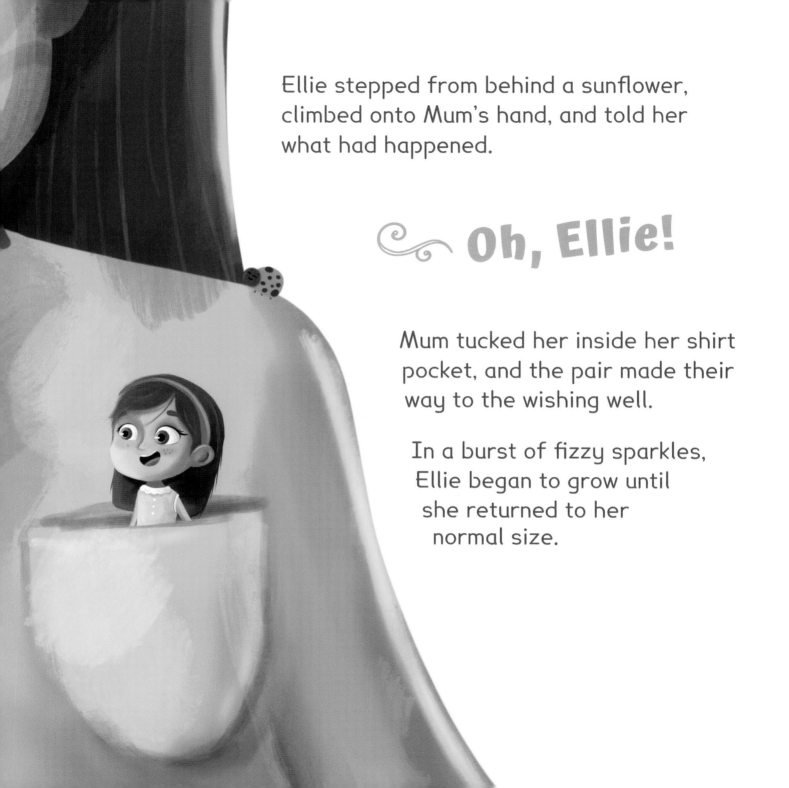

Ellie stepped from behind a sunflower, climbed onto Mum's hand, and told her what had happened.

Oh, Ellie!

Mum tucked her inside her shirt pocket, and the pair made their way to the wishing well.

In a burst of fizzy sparkles, Ellie began to grow until she returned to her normal size.

"It's important to follow your dreams," said Mum.
"But you should always be careful what you wish
for to avoid getting into trouble."

Ellie hugged her mum, and the two of them
went home to bake more cupcakes.

That evening,
as she drifted off to sleep,
Ellie couldn't help but think,

If the wishing well could make me bigger than an elephant and smaller than a mouse, surely it could also help me fly like a bird?

What a great idea!
What could possibly go wrong?!

DEAR READER,

I HOPE YOU ENJOYED READING ABOUT ELLIE AND HER TEENY-WEENY ADVENTURES! DID YOU KNOW THAT IN THE FIRST BOOK, *ELLIE AND THE CUPCAKES*, SHE GREW TO BE A GIANT?! IF YOU LIKED ELLIE SMALL, YOU'LL LOVE ELLIE TALL!

Ellie is an adventurous girl who fearlessly follows her dreams. Sometimes she gets more than she expected and things don't always work out *quite* as she had hoped, but that doesn't matter. The important thing is that she tried something new and learned from her mistakes.

I hope that after reading about Ellie, you're encouraged to follow your dreams, too.

Until next time,
Amanda.

P.S. You can download Ellie's printable board game, colouring sheets, and more! Check out **www.amandakiddstories.com/free.**

DO YOU LIKE MUSIC?

Ellie has a special song you can
listen to if you do! Grab an adult,
and listen to it here:

www.amandakiddstories.com/shop
/ellies-adventure-song

Or ask them
to scan this code!

HAVE YOU READ THESE OTHER BOOKS?

By Amanda Kidd and Noor Alshalabi

Ellie and the Cupcakes

Ellie feels like the luckiest girl in the world when her wish comes true, and she turns into a real giant. After all, when you're big, you don't have to listen to your mum! Soon, Ellie finds out being so big has unexpected challenges. Her size scares her friends and startles her mum. Worst of all, her beloved cupcakes are now incredibly tiny! Included in the book is Ellie's favourite cupcake and buttercream recipe. *YUM!*

Sam the Sneezing Scarecrow

A scarecrow has ONE job: Scare the birds.
Sam wants to do his job well. He really does. But he has a problem... He's allergic to feathers! Sam decides it's best to find another job, and that's where his adventures begin.

Kids love to follow Sam on his journey of self-discovery, acceptance, courage, and friendship, and grown-ups love the underlying message: It's hard to accept yourself, but it's the most important thing.

Pip Saves Christmas

Meet Pip. He's a kind-hearted gerbil who lives on his own in a shoe at the edge of the forest. When Twinkle the Elf shows up unexpectedly one cold Christmas Eve, Pip embarks on an exciting journey to the North Pole to try and rescue a group of elves.

Can Pip save Christmas? Will he solve the mystery of the missing cranberry sauce? And, what other surprises are in store for him? The adventures of Pip and his friends capture the Christmas spirit of selflessness that everyone craves. Enjoy a fun Christmas tale, told through the eyes of a tiny creature with a big heart.

www.amandakiddstories.com

Publisher
Cuckoo-Bye House Publishers

ISBN: 978-1-8382806-1-1
Editor: Stephanie R. Graham
Illustrator: Noor Alshalabi
Designer: Krysta Micallef

 amandakiddstories
 amanda_kidd_stories
 amandackidd